trash trucks!

Daniel Kirk

G. P. Putnam's Sons
New York

Library of Congress Cataloging-in-Publication Data
Kirk, Daniel.   Trash trucks! / Daniel Kirk.   p.   cm.
Summary: Trash trucks roam the city streets gobbling up all the garbage.
[1. Refuse and refuse disposal—Fiction. 2. Trucks—Fiction.   3. Stories in rhyme.]
I. Title.   PZ8.3.K6553Tr   1997   [E] dc20   95—47881   CIP AC
ISBN 0-399-22927-2

10 9 8 7 6 5 4 3 2 1
First Impression

Text set in 24 pt. Litterbox

Book design by Julia Gorton.

This book is for

Jonah

sssh! we said,
Sssh! Not a sound...
It's daybreak in
our dirty town.
Wildlife prowls
the grimy street;
a rumble rises
from the heat.

Are they beasts,
    or great machines
that feast to keep
        our city clean?
        There's no
            need to turn
            and flee;
        Now's our
            chance!

            Let's go
            and see...

The TRASH

trash

trash

TRUCKS! TRUCKS! TRUCKS!

Who makes a mess
at work and play?

Who bags the junk
to throw away?

We make the mess,
we put it out.

give that to us!
the trash trucks shout.

So stand back, Kim,
and watch out, Pete,
trash trucks are here—
it's time to eat!

These trucks have teeth and
claws like lions;

hear their **roar** all over town.

Mighty muscled men
have chained 'em
but fearsome hunger
drives 'em on.

Dash 'em, smash 'em,
massive jaws—
Look out! Like that—
Your trash is gone!

rattle!
Hoisting up the cans...

batter!
Out the garbage spews...

crunch!
Now that grinding sound...

PU 202

shake!
He's shaking just like you!

But stay back, kids,
safe on the curb;
don't get too close!
Do not disturb...

The
TRASH
TRASH TRASH
TRASH

TRUCKS! TRUCKS! TRUCKS!

Here's one big hungry diesel beast
chowing down his garbage feast,
   while two more snort and sniff the air
and catch the scent that's drifting there.
   The pair arrive, but it's too late...

"I'm sorry, boys, it's all been ate.
But I know where there's trash enough
   to feed a dozen rigs...."

I'll race you down to Cherry Street.

Let's go, you garbage pigs!"

Now here comes Kim with her pal Pete.
They haul their rubbish
to the street and heave it.
With a noisy crash
it lands atop the wall of trash.
But then the wiggling, jiggling heap
of garbage starts to fall.
The frightened children hear a shout—
"Look out!" the trash trucks call!

For down the road three trash trucks speed
to sound out the alarm.
They hurtle through a rain of junk
and save the kids from harm!

Three cheers, three cheers for trash trucks with their mighty jaws of steel.

rumble! Do you dare to peek?

drip! Please, please come back next week!